Magic Pony

Worst Week at School

"That's a rat trap all right," said Ned, skidding to a halt. "At the slightest touch the trap will spring."

They were only just in time, for coming down the tunnel came a beast so huge that Natty was suddenly terrified. The beast, which was of course Danny, twitched his whiskers at the sight of a girl on a pony, and tested the air with his nose.

Follow all of Natty and Ned's adventures!
Collect all the fantastic books in the
Magic Pony series:

Magic Pony

Worst Week at School

ELIZABETH LINDSAY

Illustrated by John Eastwood

SCHOLASTIC

For Rupert

Scholastic Children's Books,
Euston House, 24 Eversholt Street,
London NW1 1DB, UK
a division of Scholastic Ltd
London ~ New York ~ Toronto ~ Sydney ~ Auckland

First published in the UK by Scholastic Ltd, 1999
This edition published in the UK by Scholastic Ltd, 2005

10 digit ISBN 0 439 95974 8
13 digit ISBN 978 0439 95974 2
10 digit fairs edition ISBN 0 439 95476 2
13 digit fairs edition ISBN 978 0439 95476 1

Printed in the UK by CPI Bookmarque, Croydon, CR0 4TD

6 8 10 9 7 5

Contents

Chapter 1

The "Favourite Thing" Picture

Natty sat at the desk in her bedroom, felt-tip poised above a large sheet of white paper. She looked at the cheeky head she had drawn – two little ears, two black button eyes, a pointy nose and lots of whiskers. The body had four pink feet and a long, thin tail.

She swung round to the pony poster on the wall above her chest of drawers.

"Ned, look what I've drawn," she said. "Danny the rat!"

The pony in the poster looked out with pricked ears, his chestnut

forelock tumbling over a white blaze, but he said nothing. His limpid brown eyes stared over Natty's shoulder into a distance that was way beyond her bedroom wall. "Dear Ned, I wish your magic would work. It hasn't for ages."

"Wish whose magic would work?" The voice came from the door, not the poster, as Natty so badly wanted, and it made her jump.

"Jamie, I wish you wouldn't do that!"

"Do what?"

"Creep up on me."

 "If you didn't spend so much time talking to yourself then you'd hear me coming."

Her mouth opened to protest, but instead of saying she wasn't talking to herself, Natty said nothing.

"Besides," Jamie continued, "if you want magic then you only have to come to me. The Amazing Jamie Abracadabra Deakin – most famous magician in the whole world."

"You wish," said Natty, grinning at her brother in spite of herself.

"By the time I'm grown up I will be. Mr Cosby thinks I will. You wait and see."

"Well," said Natty, "if Mr Cosby thinks you will … then maybe."

Jamie bought all his magic tricks from Mr Cosby's shop – Cosby's Magic Emporium – and it was from there that Natty had bought the pony poster of Ned. It was a very special poster too, for when it worked, Ned's magic was quite the most wonderful thing ever. It was also Natty's biggest secret.

"Do you want to see what I've drawn?"

Jamie groaned. "Not another horse picture."

Natty held up the drawing. "It's Danny, our class rat."

"That's a change from everlasting ponies," said Jamie with surprise.

Natty glanced up at Ned's poster. So far Jamie hadn't realized there was anything special about the pony picture on her wall, and that was the way she was going to keep it.

"Oh," Jamie said, as if suddenly remembering, "Mum says you've got to hurry up, otherwise you'll miss the bus." And, message delivered, he strode from the room and bounded downstairs.

"Phew, Ned! That was a narrow squeak. When I talk to you I must remember to close my door."

Natty fetched her school rucksack and slid the drawing of Danny carefully inside before crossing to the window. On the window sill Natty's three china ponies were in a line facing her bed, and in the field opposite, Penelope Potter's pony, Pebbles, was grazing in the early morning sun.

"You shall all three look outside," she told the china ponies. "Much more fun. Esmerelda, you can look towards Winchway Wood.

Prince can look at Pebbles, and
Percy can look towards Pebbles's
stable and be the first to see me
when I come home from school.

There! I hope you have an interesting
day and think up lots of pretends for
yourselves. I'd like to think up a
pretend with Ned but I simply
haven't got time."

Then, with a quick goodbye, she picked up her rucksack and raced from the room.

Natty didn't have time for a proper pretend on the school bus either. She hurried to a free seat, eager to start one, while Jamie went to the back of the bus to join his friends. After saying hello, Penelope Potter sat down in front of her and saved a place for her best friend, Trudi. The pretend had got as far as Natty climbing on to Ned's back and her magic riding clothes appearing when the bus drew up at Trudi's stop.

By the time Ned had gone from being as large as Pebbles to becoming as small as china pony Percy, which he would if his magic were truly working, Trudi and Penelope were leaning over the backs of their seats. Although Natty wanted to keep on being a tiny person riding along the window sill, it was impossible with two nosy faces peering round at her.

"Haven't you two got anything better to do than stare at me?" Natty asked.

"We're only being friendly," said Penelope.

Trudi's face stretched into one of her elastic smiles. "We want to see your picture."

Natty was instantly on guard, not wanting her drawing to get crumpled or torn.

"I'm not getting it out now," she said. "The bus is juddering all over the place. You'll have to wait until school."

Trudi's smile almost reached her ears. "Oh, come on, Natty. We know how good you are at drawing."

"Especially, 'specially good," chimed in Penelope.

"Yes, so pleeeease show us."

"No, show me yours first and I might," Natty said.

"Go on, Penelope." Trudi gave her friend a nudge.

"No," said Penelope. "You show yours first."

"You know I can't. I didn't do a very good one."

"Well I don't see why I should," complained Penelope.

Both girls slid down into their seats bickering. Natty breathed a sigh of relief. Best not to give in to those two. You could never tell what might happen. She tried continuing with the pretend but couldn't concentrate, and it faded away. Instead she thought of what lay ahead once the bus arrived at school.

This week they were beginning a project on "What We Do In School", in preparation for parents' day, and Mr Beamish had asked them all to draw a picture of something they particularly liked about school. The best pictures would go in the display.

Natty had thought of drawing Danny sitting on their teacher's shoulder – which he loved to do when Mr Beamish was writing on the blackboard – but in the end she didn't. She had filled her paper with a large picture of Danny by himself and was desperate to see it pinned up, knowing Mum and Dad would love it. She tucked her hand protectively around her school rucksack.

This was just as well because creeping fingers had taken hold of the strap and the rucksack was almost pulled from her grasp. She wrenched it back again.

"Ouch! That hurt."

"What do you think you're doing, Trudi? Just leave my things alone."

"You could have broken my arm,

Natalie Deakin. Now I've got a bruise."

The bus drew up outside the school gates and the door opened. Natty seized her chance for a quick getaway.

"You were stealing my rucksack," she cried, flinging the words over her shoulder. "But I didn't mean to hurt your arm!"

It was always the same with Trudi, if she didn't get her own way, she'd just take things. So before there could be any more unpleasantness, Natty jumped on to the tarmac and hurried off in search of her best friend, Robyn.

Chapter 2
Teacher Shock

Robyn was waiting for Natty on the bench in their special place under the maple tree, her nose in a book, as usual. At Natty's approach she looked up, her welcoming grin fading when she saw the expression on Natty's face.

"What's up?" she asked, shoving

the book into her school bag.

"It's Trudi, as usual. She tried stealing my rucksack to sneak a look at my picture. She says I bruised her arm. But I didn't mean to."

"Typical! At least she didn't get it." Robyn patted the bench beside her and Natty sat down. "Did you draw Danny, like you said?" Natty carefully took out her picture.

"It's perfect," said Robyn. "Just like him. I can almost see his whiskers twitching. I bet that gets in the display."

"With luck," said Natty. "What did you do?"

As Robyn was passionate about reading, Natty expected a picture with books in it. But when she looked at what Robyn had drawn, it was so different from what she imagined, she burst out laughing.

There was a classroom with a book teacher and book pupils, each with little arms and legs sticking out from their book bodies. Underneath the story titles on the covers, Robyn had painted jolly faces, and all the book people held tiny reading books.

"Brilliant, Robs. Mr Beamish'll love that."

"I hope so. There's a book person for each of us in the class and it took ages. I printed all my favourite titles on the covers."

The bell went and they tucked their pictures back into their rucksacks and hurried into school. They were on their way into the classroom when they bumped into Penelope and Trudi.

"Your arm OK?" Natty asked.

"No, thanks to you," said Trudi with a frown, and shoved her way in front to burst in first through the classroom door, which was, as it turned out, a mistake.

Waiting by the teacher's table was a tall, stern-looking lady, with wispy grey hair pulled back in a bun. She looked down at Trudi and wrinkled her nose as if the girl was something smelly. Next to this forbidding lady stood Mrs Smedley, their head teacher. Entering the classroom, the pupils fell silent one by one, turning to shush the others following.

The class stared at the stranger with wide eyes as they filed to their places. Where was Mr Beamish? The stranger stared back, her quick eyes darting from one pupil to the next. This was no longer an ordinary morning and while the class waited for their head

teacher's explanation, Natty had the awful feeling that something horrid was about to happen. Mrs Smedley cleared her throat.

"Good morning, Class B."

"Good morning, Mrs Smedley."

"I'd like to introduce you to Miss Pike, who has kindly come in to teach you as Mr Beamish will be away this week."

There was a muted groan. Miss Pike's beady eyes glinted and her long neck seemed to sway. A hush fell at once. "Now, I'm sure you'll make Miss Pike feel at home, Class B, and that you'll have an enjoyable week."

"Thank you, Mrs Smedley," said Miss Pike, smiling politely while waiting for the head teacher to leave. The moment the classroom door closed, Miss Pike said, "Sit!" The class sat. "Not like that. Not like that. No scraping of chairs. Lift them. Lift them."

Everyone sat as quietly as possible and tried not to move a muscle.

Natty turned briefly to Robyn and pulled an *isn't-this-terrible* face. A flicker of panic signalled in Robyn's eyes but she was too late.

"You girl. Yes, you. Stand up."

Natty swallowed. Miss Pike was pointing at her. Slowly she stood up.

"Name?"

"Natty."

"Natty? What sort of a name is that? Full name. Out with it."

"Natalie Deakin."

"Very well, Natalie Deakin. Let it be understood that from this moment on we have no pulling of faces in this room by you or any other member of this class. Remain standing. You, now you stand up." This time the finger was pointing at Trudi. "You. The girl who pushed her way so rudely into class. Up. Up. Name?"

"Trudi Tyler."

"Trudi Tyler. And pray tell, Trudi

Tyler, what required such an ill-mannered entry into the peaceful domain of this pleasant classroom?" Trudi stepped backwards into her chair, making it scrape, and Miss Pike's eyes bulged from their sockets.

"I… I… I…" stuttered Trudi.

"Out with it, child!" But Trudi was so frightened by Miss Pike's wild stare that she could not manage another word.

"It was my fault," said Natty, jumping in to save the situation.

"Your fault?" Miss Pike's beady gaze landed on Natty and she folded her arms. "Then explain, Natalie Deakin. I am waiting."

Natty took in a deep breath. "On the school bus Trudi's arm somehow got hurt, which made her cross, and she came into class a bit fast."

"Are you trying to tell me that

you deliberately harmed Trudi?"

"No, no, not deliberately. Trudi wanted to see the picture I'd drawn for Mr Beamish and I didn't want to show it. Her arm got hurt by mistake."

"A picture for Mr Beamish? Bring it to me at once."

Reluctantly, Natty pulled out the drawing of Danny. Miss Pike held out her hand. "I will not have squabbling in my class, Natalie Deakin, as you will find out."

Natty walked slowly to the front of the class and offered up the picture.

Miss Pike shook the paper and peered at the drawing. Then she gave Natty one of her wrinkled-nose looks and turned the paper the other way up as if it was Natty's fault she was looking at the picture upside down.

But when she looked at it the right way up, her nose wrinkled even more and she held out the paper at arm's length as if it was something quite disgusting.

Trying not to move a muscle, Natty held her breath, and so it seemed did everyone else in the class. Then, through the silence, came the scrabble-scrabble sound of tiny feet rustling in paper.

"Who is making that noise?" demanded Miss Pike.

"It's Danny," said Natty.

"Stand up, Daniel, at once!"

"No, no, look," said Natty and ran to the back of the classroom, where she lifted the lid from a glass cage and rummaged in a nest of shredded paper. "This is who my picture's of." And she proudly carried Danny to the front of the room. "He's Class B's brown rat and it's my turn to look after him this week."

Danny, who had just woken from a satisfying sleep, twitched his nose, wiggled his whiskers and looked Miss Pike straight in the eye.

Miss Pike turned to stone, or so it appeared, and her spectacles slid down her nose.

There was a moment of terrible silence. Then, quite unexpectedly, she jumped on to the teacher's chair. "Vermin!" she cried, waving them away with Natty's picture. "Filthy vermin. Put it back in its cage at once."

Natty hurried to obey, clutching the startled Danny, who wriggled to escape. She managed to get him back into the cage, where he squeezed from her clutches and burrowed into the safety of his nest. Natty quickly put back the lid and turned her own pale face towards the new teacher, aware that Miss Pike's squinting eyes followed her every move.

"Do not remove that creature from its cage again. Do you understand?"

"Yes, Miss Pike."

The teacher stepped down from the chair, fanning herself with the picture. "In my opinion the only good rat is a dead..." She caught sight of the sea of shocked faces and didn't finish. "Gracious me, we must get on. Time and tide wait for no one."

Then, with a little shiver, she ripped Natty's picture into tiny pieces and dropped the bits into the bin. The class was stunned. Natty had the dreadful feeling that if Miss Pike wasn't so scared of Danny, she would have ripped him to pieces as well. "Sit, Trudi Tyler." Trudi crumpled into her place.

There was a deathly hush while the class waited for what was coming next.

"Natalie Deakin, go and wash your hands, and use plenty of soap. Get rid of all those disgusting rat germs."

Miss Pike tapped her bun to make sure it was still in place before curling her lips into a smile. But everyone could see that her eyes were as piercing as ever.

"Now, Class B, take out your English books. You are going to show me how well you can write."

Natty slunk to the sink at the back of the classroom and turned on the tap. She could hardly believe that her wonderful picture lay shredded at the bottom of the waste-paper bin. And worse, poor Danny must be as frightened as she was, and there was nothing she could do to comfort him.

Chapter 3
Rat Escape

At breaktime Class B gathered in the playground in unusually subdued and whispering groups. They took this opportunity to say how sorry they were that Natty's picture was torn up. Even Trudi, who looked horribly pale and kept leaning on Penelope as if she was going to faint.

"It's when she looks at you," Trudi groaned. "Her eyes bore right into you."

"She must be the worst teacher in the world to tear up such a good drawing," said Robyn. "I saw the picture and it was brilliant."

"She's the teacher from hell," muttered Penelope. "Mr Beamish'd better come back soon, that's all I can say."

It was Natty who was most worried. "The worst thing is, she hates rats, and Danny's all on his own in the classroom with no one to protect him."

"But what can she do to him?" asked Robyn. "He's our class pet."

"Poison him," said Penelope. "I bet she's the sort of person who carries rat poison around in her handbag."

"She wouldn't," said Natty. "Would she?"

Yet when everyone filed back into

class after playtime, they found
Miss Pike patrolling up and down
the classroom, smacking a ruler on
to tabletops in between ducking to
look at the floor.

Natty and Robyn noticed at once that the lid was half off Danny's cage and exchanged anxious glances.

"Sit!" said Miss Pike.

Carefully lifting their chairs, Class B sat.

"Own up," said Miss Pike, turning on them at once. "Which of you has removed the rat from its cage?"

Her accusation was met by shocked murmurs and wide-eyed, disbelieving faces. Natty put up her hand.

"So it was you, Natalie Deakin? I might have guessed."

"No, no. I just wanted to say that Danny might have pushed the lid off."

"And why would that be? Because the stupid girl who put him back in his cage didn't put the lid back on properly."

"No, I did put the lid back on properly. It's just that usually by now Danny's had lots of exercise in his rat run."

"His rat run?" huffed Miss Pike. "What's that?"

Natty pointed to the back of the classroom. Miss Pike turned her stare to a series of gaily painted cardboard tubes and boxes decorated with flowers, birds and butterflies that ran along the rear wall and under the window.

"The boxes and tubes are his rat run. They're all connected. Mr Beamish lets Danny run up and down

inside it all day if he wants to. He could be in it now, for all we know."

Miss Pike scuttled to the front of the class and stood on her chair brandishing her ruler. "Search the room, Class B! Pick up those boxes and shake the rodent out. It must be found."

"But if we shake the rat run, it might break," said Natty.

"I don't care."

No one moved a muscle until Miss Pike smashed her ruler down on the table and shrieked, "GET A MOVE ON!"

Suddenly everyone in Class B was scuttling hither and thither, looking up tubes and shaking boxes, crawling under tables and searching behind books on bookshelves. Natty carefully checked Danny's nest to make sure it was empty, then got down beside Robyn under a table.

"I'm sure I put the lid back on properly," she whispered.

Robyn glanced over her shoulder. "Miss Pike could be making it up about Danny's escape. She could have done what Penelope said and poisoned him."

"Oh, this is terrible," groaned Natty. "What will we tell Mr Beamish when he comes back? He really loves Danny."

After all the searching, the rat run had come apart in the middle and it was a very sad Class B who finally had to admit defeat and say they couldn't find their special pet.

"Very well," said Miss Pike. "Class, sit! Lessons must go on in spite of this outrage. Take out your maths books. We are here to work, Class B, not waste time. And wasting time is what we have been doing."

Looking warily at the floor, Miss Pike stepped down from her chair. "A rat is a rat. For the present, let it roam. It won't bother me."

Natty took out her maths book and thought that if Miss Pike expected them to believe that, she was not very good at pretending. The teacher's gaze kept darting to the floor and she had a tight hold of the ruler.

"I don't think she has poisoned him," whispered Natty. "She's too frightened."

"Let's hope you're right," Robyn whispered back.

Ages later, after lots of hard work, there was still no sign of Danny and Natty had writer's cramp. She had done all the sums and was certain that she had the right answers. It was Robyn who was struggling miserably. Natty leant across the table, longing to help. Mr Beamish always let her when Robyn was stuck.

"Natalie Deakin, what are you doing?" Miss Pike advanced towards her tapping the ruler into her palm.

"I think Robyn needs some help," said Natty.

"If Robyn cannot do the work by

herself then she must put up her hand. Do you need help, Robyn?"

"Yes, no, well sort of."

"Either you do or you don't. Speak up, girl."

"Yes," said Robyn. "I'm stuck. It's really difficult." And under Miss Pike's stern gaze she burst into tears.

"Oh, for goodness' sake, stop that unnecessary snivelling and sit up," snapped Miss Pike.

Natty pulled a tissue from her pocket and passed it to her friend. "I don't think it's fair to make Robyn cry when she's trying her hardest. No one ever cries when Mr Beamish is here." There was an eerie silence while Miss Pike turned her stony gaze on Natty.

"Natalie Deakin," said the oily voice. "If you dare to speak to me like that again, you will be severely punished. I can think of several ways to make your life extremely unpleasant." Miss Pike brought her face down until Natty became almost cross-eyed looking at the point of her nose. "Do you understand, Natalie?"

Natty didn't dare move a muscle. "Yes, Miss Pike."

"You are a troublemaker and I do not like troublemakers. The sooner you mend your ways the better." The bell rang. "And just to show you that

I mean what I say, you can spend your lunchtime in here looking for the rat." Miss Pike glanced nervously at the floor. "Do I make myself clear, Natalie?"

"Yes, Miss Pike."

"Books away! Class B, you are dismissed."

When everyone but Natty had filed from the classroom, Miss Pike hurried to go too, turning back in time to say, "Don't just sit there, Natalie. Start looking!" before slamming the door.

"Danny, Danny, where are you?" called Natty and began another hopeless search. In the end she took out her lunch box and scattered bits of tomato sandwich at one end of the rat run, hoping to tempt Danny out, although really she knew he wasn't in there. She ate the rest before deciding to look one more time. She was on her hands and knees peering down a cardboard tube when Mrs Smedley found her.

"Oh, Natty, dear, have you found him?"

"No," cried Natty. "It's terrible! Miss Pike hates rats, and what'll Mr Beamish say?"

"Don't worry, he'll turn up. He can't have gone far. You go and join your friends in the playground and I'll have a look."

"Miss Pike says I'm to stay here," said Natty.

"I'll tell Miss Pike I gave you permission, and if I find Danny, I'll take him to my office."

Later, when they came back to class, it was obvious Mrs Smedley hadn't found Danny, for his cage was still empty at the back of the classroom. Miss Pike placed her chair on the teacher's table and, clutching her ruler, sat at this great height for the rest of the afternoon, glaring down at the class and issuing orders.

When the bell rang she quickly
dismissed everybody, jumped to

the floor and hurried from the classroom. Natty hung back. After all it was her turn to clean and feed Danny this week and she wanted to have one last look.

"You'll miss your bus," said Robyn.

"Danny's in here somewhere. I just want to find him."

"He's done the most sensible thing," said Robyn. "He's found somewhere really safe and out of Miss Pike's way. If he's really clever, he'll stay there till Mr Beamish gets back next week."

"But if we find him, we could take him to Mrs Smedley's office. He'd be safe there."

"We haven't got time," said Robyn. "If we don't hurry, we'll both miss our buses." And she took hold of Natty's arm and pulled her from the classroom.

Chapter 4
Ned Comes to School

It wasn't until after tea that Natty was finally able to shut her bedroom door, sit on the bed next to the furry, fast-asleep bundle that was Tabitha, her cat, and have a proper talk to the pony in the poster on her wall. She poured out the disastrous story of how Mr Beamish was unexpectedly away and how instead the class had Miss Pike, a teacher so horrid that she had torn up her drawing of Danny.

"But most dreadful of all is that Danny has escaped," Natty groaned. "Miss Pike hates rats. If she finds him before we do, she might do something terrible."

She gazed up at the pony in the poster and although he was still a smooth, shiny picture pony, he looked as if he had heard every word.

There was a knock and Dad popped his head round the door.

"It's time you were putting on your pyjamas," he said. "It's getting late. I'll be back in ten minutes to say goodnight."

When she lay tucked up in bed with Tabitha curled on her feet, Natty closed her eyes and wished her hardest.

"Please, Ned, let your magic work tomorrow," she begged. "You haven't been out of your poster for ages and you'd know what to do about Miss Pike." Then, with a little sigh, she turned over and, trying not to think of the horrible new teacher, closed her eyes.

It took ages to get to sleep, and when she did, she tossed and turned, tumbling into a dark dream where she found herself in a room stacked high with great sacks labelled RAT POISON. Natty knew at once she was in a cellar under the school. Footsteps echoed around her and she tried to hide but found she couldn't move. A tall figure towered over her and turned into Miss Pike. Natty was scared. From beneath a flowing cloak, the teacher took out a small glass cage.

She thought the cage was empty but Miss Pike's triumphant smile made Natty look again. Inside was Danny the rat.

"Natty," called Danny, scrabbling at the sides. "Help me!"

Natty tried to snatch him but Miss Pike laughed and held the cage out of reach.

"You, Natalie, you are going to feed him the poison."

"No," Natty cried. "No, I won't."

"Natty," called the rat again, and this time when she stretched out to reach him, she floated away from the dark cellar and Danny was left behind. Another voice whispered her name, but so softly that at first she didn't hear it.

"Danny," she sobbed. "Danny, where are you?"

"Natty, wake up. It's me, Ned. You've had a bad dream."

Gentle pony lips brushed away the tears on her cheek. Natty rolled over and opened her eyes. There, beside the bed, filling up all the space between the door and the wall, was her magic pony.

"Ned," she cried. "Oh, Ned, you've come out of your picture at last."

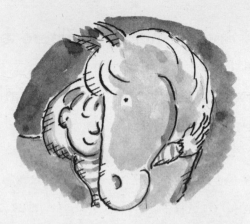

And she flung her arms about his neck and buried her face in his chestnut mane.

"There, there," said Ned. "It was only a dream." And he nuzzled her close. "Tell me all about it."

"It was Miss Pike, in a cellar under the school, and she was going to poison Danny. We've got to find him before she does. We've got to, Ned."

"And we shall," said Ned. "But first you must get up."

Tabitha was still fast asleep but the sun, peeping in through the crack in the curtains, announced it was morning. Natty felt much better now that Ned had come out of his poster, even though the moment she put her feet on the carpet, the magic wind blew and he was gone. She knew he wouldn't be far away, and dropped down on her hands and knees to look.

There, in front of her, galloped a

tiny chestnut pony, his mane and tail flying wildly just as if he were the china Percy come to life. Ned twisted and turned, took a flying leap over one of Natty's trainers and came to a prancing stop before her.

"Hurry up," he said. "We're going to get to school early."

"But what about the bus?"

"You don't need the bus when you can ride me!"

"Ned!" Natty's eyes shone. "I'll be ready in two ticks, but I'll have to have breakfast, otherwise Mum'll wonder what's going on."

"Of course," said Ned. "I shall wait in your rucksack."
He trotted across the carpet and jumped into the front pocket. "Now hurry up. Oh, and bring a torch. We may need it."

Natty didn't need telling twice. She added her pocket torch to the things in her rucksack and was washed, dressed and racing downstairs in no time, surprising Mum with her early start. She ate some toast, collected her lunch box and grabbed her rucksack.

"See you later, Mum," she called and was gone.

Natty was hurrying past Penelope's stable yard when Ned said, "In here." The yard was empty, and as soon as they were out of sight behind the hedge, Ned jumped from the rucksack, landing proper pony size beside her, wearing his saddle and bridle, ready for her to mount.

Natty took hold of the reins and sprang on to his back. As soon as she was in the saddle, her school clothes vanished and she was dressed in a velvet hard hat, hacking jacket, jodhpurs and jodhpur boots.

Her rucksack was transformed into a pair of saddlebags, which hung across Ned's back. Wearing the magic riding clothes was her perfect disguise. No one would recognize her as Natalie Deakin now. Natty adjusted her chinstrap and was ready to go.

"Hold tight," cried Ned.

Natty expected him to turn into the lane but instead he cantered towards the field, leaping the gate before galloping by the surprised Pebbles who, just a moment before, had been quietly grazing. The dappled grey pony kicked up his heels and galloped alongside until Ned leapt the further hedge, leaving Pebbles to watch them go.

"Ned, where are we going?" Natty cried. "Straight to school across country. It's the quickest way for a horse."

The speed was thrilling. Natty stood in her stirrups and counted strides at each hedge and ditch they leapt while the wind whistled and her eyes watered. What a way to come to school, she thought, and wished she could ride there like this every day.

Before she realized it, Ned was galloping across the deserted playing field. It looked as though they were early enough to have the school to themselves.

"We'll take a peep in your classroom window," said Ned, "and then we'll decide what to do."

Natty lay low on Ned's neck while he crept beside the wall.

"Look," she said, noticing one of the windows wasn't properly shut. "If I pulled that open, we could get in there."

Natty stood in her stirrups and leant up Ned's neck, and together they

peered into the classroom to make
sure it was empty. Only it wasn't.

"It's Miss Pike," Natty gasped.

"So that's her, is it?" whispered
Ned. "She's up to something."

Miss Pike was wearing pink rubber
gloves and holding
some kind of
gadget.

And, as they watched, she stuck what looked like a chunk of yellow cheese on to the gadget before placing it in the broken part of Danny's rat run.

"It's a trap," said Ned.

"A rat trap?" Natty was horrified. "I knew she'd do something like this."

Next, Miss Pike pulled out a roll of sticky tape and spent several minutes taping up the cardboard. At last she appeared satisfied and pulled off the pink gloves. She stuffed both gloves and tape in her handbag then, with a quick look over her shoulder, hurried from the classroom.

"We must be quick," said Ned. "Danny'll smell the cheese in no time. For a hungry rat, a piece that size is a feast. We must get there before he does."

"Let's go!" cried Natty, and leaning over, pulled the window wide. Ned turned in a circle and galloped towards the opening. He took a mighty leap into a blast of magic wind while Natty clung on and closed her eyes.

Chapter 5
Rat Trap

They landed inside on the window sill, a tiny pony and a tiny rider in what seemed like a giant's classroom. Natty was amazed at the hugeness of it, but Ned wasted no time and jumped to the top of the bookshelf.

"What we need is a pencil," he cried.

"I've got one in my pencil case," said Natty.

"Good thinking," said Ned, skidding to a stop while Natty undid the buckle on one of the saddlebags. She found her pencil case and took out a pencil.

"That tiny size won't be any good," said Ned as Natty rebuckled the saddlebag. He manoeuvred himself next to a pile of books. "Put the pencil on top here and let go."

Natty did as she was told, and in a jiffy the miniature pencil became its proper size, which seemed gigantic to her.

"What's it for?" she asked.

"It's to make a lance. Can you pick it up?"

Natty wrapped her arm around the pencil and lifted it.

"Just about."

"Good. You're going to spring the rat trap with it."

Ned trotted to the end of the bookcase and Natty leant back, holding on tightly to the pencil, as Ned dropped to the table below. They hit the shiny top and began to slide. The edge came closer and closer and, realizing they weren't going to stop, Natty swung the pencil rubber to the tabletop and used it as a brake.

"Well done," cried Ned, sorting out his feet at last before jumping on to a chair and taking a final leap to the floor.

Natty breathed a sigh of relief and tucked the pencil back under her arm while Ned set off at a gallop, racing between the table and chair legs to the place in the rat run where Miss Pike had set the trap. They arrived panting to find that sticky tape completely covered the hole and they couldn't get in. Not even when Natty prodded the tape with the pencil point.

Wasting no time, Ned turned on his haunches and galloped for the nearest rat run entrance, racing past a jungle of flowers and butterflies spreading high above them before trotting into the dark. Now they were inside, Natty let go of the reins and fumbled in one of the saddlebags for her torch.

"Listen," said Ned. "I can hear something."

Echoing down the tube came a distant pitter-patter of clawed feet.

"It's Danny!" whispered Natty. "He must have come in at the other end."

"Yes," agreed Ned. "Heading straight for the cheese."

They had no time to lose. Holding on tightly to the pencil with one hand, Natty shone the torch with the other, leaving the steering to Ned. With reins flying, the pony flew down the tunnel, galloping into a cavern of a box.

"Now where?" he asked, champing at the bit.

There were three tubes running off the far side of the box, but Natty was sure the top two tubes doubled back on themselves.

"Down there," she said, pointing the torch, hoping she was right. This tube twisted and turned. The class had made it like this on purpose so it would be more fun for Danny – but it slowed down his rescuers.

"If I've remembered it right, the break's through one more box and into the next tube," said Natty.

Ned raced across the floor of the next large box and, guided by the torch beam, sped into the tube opposite.

"There it is," cried Natty as the torch lit up an innocent-looking yellow lump the size of a hefty rock, which lay in their path.

"That's a rat trap all right," said Ned, skidding to a halt. "At the slightest touch the trap will spring.

They were only just in time, for coming down the tunnel from the other direction came a beast so huge that Natty was suddenly terrified.

The beast, which was of course Danny, twitched his whiskers at the sight of a girl on a pony, and tested the air with his nose.

"Lance the cheese, Natty," shouted

Ned, prancing forwards. "Before he comes any closer." Natty took aim. She thrust the pencil into the cheese and let go. The trap snapped, splintering the pencil into pieces. Stunned by the noise, none of them moved until Natty swung round in the saddle.

"Danny, it's nothing to worry about," she called, hoping he would recognize her voice.

The rat blinked twice, and unable to resist the cheese, reached out with his front paws and pulled it from its spike.

Transferring it to his mouth, he pattered off with his prize.

Natty highlighted the remains of the pencil. "That could have been Danny," she said.

"Indeed," replied Ned. "All thanks to Miss Pike. We must get after him and find out where he's hiding."

Stepping round the trap, Ned set off in pursuit and they followed the pitter-patter of Danny's feet, catching the occasional glimpse of his tail in the torchlight. At last they came out into a large box in time to see Danny disappear through a jagged hole in the cardboard.

"This isn't the end of the run," said Natty. "Danny must have chewed a way out."

They slipped through the hole, following Danny behind Mr Beamish's book cupboard. Here they discovered another rat-sized entrance.

"This must be his secret hiding place," said Natty.

Danny didn't try and stop them coming in, but sat back on his haunches nibbling hungrily, keeping a watchful eye on them as if to say, *This cheese is all mine.*

Natty's heart was pounding. Being as tiny as they were made Danny seem enormous, more like a hairy monster than the friendly brown rat she knew.

"Don't be frightened, Natty. He knows who you are," said Ned. "And he's the same old Danny."

"Yes," said Natty. "Of course he is." She put out a hand to stroke his fur. "Oh, Danny, I'm so glad we've found you. When you've finished your breakfast, we'll think what to do next."

The school bell rang, which made Natty jump.

"There's no need to worry," said Ned, lifting his nose to look over a pile of books. "We're quite safe in this cupboard, and we can stay hidden here all day if we have to."

Natty relaxed, watching the lump of cheese grow smaller until she heard the sharp tones of Miss Pike's voice. It sent a chill right through her.

"Come in, Class B, and stand at your chairs."

There was a swish of footsteps and a rustle of school bags being put on the floor, then silence. "Sit, and do it quietly!" There was none of the expectant murmur heard when Mr Beamish was their teacher.

"And pray tell, where is that troublemaker Natalie Deakin this morning?" The class remained silent. "Hands up!"

"Please, Miss Pike."

"WAIT UNTIL YOU ARE SPOKEN TO, PENELOPE." There was another pause, then Miss Pike's pretending-to-be-nice voice. "Yes, Penelope?"

"Natalie wasn't on the school bus this morning, Miss Pike."

"So she missed the bus, did she? It doesn't surprise me. But no doubt we shall have a more peaceful day without her. Take out your maths books, Class B. Robyn, your sums were a disgrace. If there's no improvement this morning, you will stay in at playtime and

lunchtime and do them all again.
Do you understand?"

"Yes, Miss Pike."
At the sound of Robyn's hurt

voice Natty grew hot with rage. "It's not Robyn's fault. She tries really hard," Natty whispered. "Miss Pike is revolting."

"Yes," said Ned. "She certainly is."

With the cheese gone, Danny licked his paws and washed his whiskers. From the silence of the classroom came the familiar pat and scrape of chalk on the blackboard. The rat pricked up his ears. Then, without warning, he brushed past them and jumped from the back of the cupboard.

"Oh, Ned! When Mr Beamish writes on the blackboard, Danny likes to sit on his shoulder."

"Well, if he sits on Miss Pike's shoulder, it might be the very thing to frighten her off."

Ned squeezed between some books and they both peered out through a crack in the door to see Miss Pike busy writing up sums and Danny scuttling purposefully across the classroom floor towards her.

Chapter 6
Teacher Scare

The chalk squeak-squeaked on the blackboard.

"Write down these sums in your best writing, Class B. You have ten minutes to do them." Miss Pike wrote up more and more sums, and the chalk kept squeaking.

"It's not fair," said Natty. "Robyn

will never be able to do that lot in ten minutes."

Danny reached the teacher's table. He jumped for the chair and hauled himself up.

"Ned, I've got to get out of this cupboard before something terrible happens."

"Agreed," said Ned.

With a huge leap Danny flew through the air and landed halfway up the back of Miss Pike's woollen dress, where he clung on.

Miss Pike swung round to face the class. "Who threw that?" she roared.

Most of the class had seen Danny and there was a shocked and deathly hush. When he arrived on Miss Pike's shoulder, the teacher slowly turned her head and came eyeball to eyeball with him. She let out a loud scream, and Danny, realizing his mistake, jumped for the table.

"Vermin!" Miss Pike shrieked. "Kill it! Kill it!"

She hit out with her ruler. Thwack! Thwack! Danny dodged, and on the third thwack the ruler snapped. He leapt from the table and raced across the floor. Seeing him go, Miss Pike grasped the nearest thing, her handbag, and threw it at him.

The attack was too much for Class B. "Leave Danny alone!" they cried, and soon Miss Pike was being pelted with pens and maths books, pencil cases and rubbers.

"Now's your chance, Natty," said Ned. The pony swung round and jumped through the hole in the back of the cupboard and galloped behind the rat run. "You can get off now. Leave the rucksack here for me to hide in," he cried.

"How dare you side with a rodent!" Miss Pike screamed above

the uproar. "How dare you throw things at me!"

Natty quickly dismounted but kept hold of the reins. The corner space she was in seemed huge, but she realized it was best to crouch down on her hands and knees before letting go. The magic wind blew and she found herself squashed between the wall and the rat run, back in her school clothes, with just enough room to pull off her rucksack. She propped it up for the tiny Ned and he jumped into the front pocket.

"Danny's safe," he called. "He's gone back in the cupboard."

What a relief! But for Natty there was no going back. Although safely out of sight behind the rat run, she knew what she was going to do. Keeping on her hands and knees, she scuttled from behind the run and under her table.

Slowly the uproar faded. Natty knew why when she heard Mrs Smedley's stern voice say, "Class B, go to your seats at once."

The moment Robyn sat down, Natty tapped her on the knee. Natty knew she'd be surprised but, to Robyn's credit, she didn't utter a sound. Instead she watched Natty make a cutting signal and, without drawing attention to herself, pulled her pointy scissors from her bag and handed them over.

"Perhaps you would explain to me what is going on, Miss Pike?" Mrs Smedley asked.

"They set the rat on me," said Miss Pike, huffing and puffing. "I have never known such an unruly, ill-disciplined class. The creature climbed up my back. I could have had heart failure. Naturally, I screamed, as you do when you find a rat on your shoulder. Then they threw things at me."

"I see," said Mrs Smedley. Natty scuttled to the back of the classroom.

Several of the others had seen her now but she put a finger to her lips and, although surprised, no one said anything.

Natty reached the taped-up place in the rat run and pushed in the scissors. It was easy now, and soon she had the hole cut open. She felt inside.

"It's a conspiracy," said Miss Pike. "Class B should be severely punished, every last one of them."

Natty wrapped her fingers round the trap and stood up.

"Please, Mrs Smedley, Miss Pike set this in Danny's run." And she held up the rat trap for everyone to see.

"Natalie Deakin!" screeched Miss Pike, her eyes popping with shocked surprise. "Where did you spring from?"

"And she wore pink rubber gloves when she was doing it," said Natty. "And stuck the rat run up with tape. But I sprang it with a pencil so it wouldn't work. The rubber gloves are in her handbag."

Miss Pike looked round quickly for her bag. It lay open on the floor, where she had thrown it, and strewn in front of it, where they had fallen, were two pink rubber gloves.

"I see," said Mrs Smedley. "Does anyone know where Danny is?"

"I do," said Natty. "I found his hiding place this morning." She longed to say, "with help from my friend Ned", but didn't.

"I came to school early. That's when I saw Miss Pike set the trap."

There was an astonished gasp from the class and Miss Pike's eyes narrowed dangerously. Natty was glad Mrs Smedley was there. "That girl tells lies. Don't believe a word of it, Mrs Smedley. She's a nasty, spying little toad."

Mrs Smedley looked at Natty's

earnest face, and turned to the teacher by her side.

"Come to my office, please, Miss Pike," she said. "And Natty, find Danny and put him back in his cage. The rest of you, sit quietly until I come back."

With a toss of her head, Miss Pike picked up her bag and the rubber gloves, and marched from the classroom. Mrs Smedley followed.

After that, sitting quietly was impossible.

"Did you spy on her?" Trudi asked. "I wish I'd thought of that."

"I wish I'd thought of getting to school early," said Penelope.

"Look, let Natty fetch Danny before you ask loads of questions," said Robyn.

Natty grinned. "Let's be really quiet so we don't frighten him," she said, and undid Mr Beamish's

book cupboard.
Taking out the
books at the
front, she found
Danny crouched
in a corner at the back. He seemed
relieved to see her, and she picked
him up and held him close.

"Poor Danny. You've had quite an
adventure." Natty cuddled him all
the way to his cage and gently put
him inside. He gave a quick twitch
of his whiskers before scampering to
his nest and burrowing out of sight.
Natty put the lid on and, to make
sure it wouldn't come off again,

placed three large books on top of it. After which she found herself bombarded with questions so, without mentioning Ned, she explained everything as best she could. It was a relief when Mrs Smedley came back into the classroom.

"Sit down, everyone, and listen." The class scooted to their places. "Miss Pike will not be coming back…" There was a gasp of delight. Mrs Smedley held up her hand for quiet. "…and I've just had a rather special phone call from Mr Beamish. It's good news. Last night his wife had a baby daughter – Alice Louise.

He's bringing a photograph to show you next week." A burst of applause and a mighty cheer followed this announcement. "In the meantime you'll have to make do with me for your form teacher."

Natty grinned with relief and Robyn grinned back. No more Miss Pike. Things were looking up. Robyn put up her hand.

"Please, Mrs Smedley, can everyone sign my book picture so we can send it to say happy birthday to Alice Louise from Class B."

"I think that's a lovely idea," said Mrs Smedley. "Let's do that straight away."

Natty fetched her rucksack.

Checking in the front pocket, she glimpsed a chestnut mane and tail. Her magic pony was safe. Now there was nothing left to do but enjoy school again and, yes, draw a new picture of Danny. She took out her pencil case.

At the end of the day, when the school bus arrived at their stop, Natty said goodbye to Penelope.

Then, to avoid any more of Jamie's awkward questions about why she hadn't been on the morning bus, she ran all the way home. Once indoors, she said a quick "hi" to her mum and rushed upstairs. Then, closing her bedroom door she put her rucksack on the floor. With a leap the tiny chestnut Ned landed on the carpet.

"I don't think Jamie believed me when I said I rode to school."

"He certainly didn't when you said it was on a horse." Ned laughed.

Outside there were footsteps on the landing and the door burst open. In the blink of an eye, the pony was gone.

"OK, Jamie, now what do you want?" asked Natty.

"Mum's just told me you left early enough to walk," said Jamie triumphantly. "So now I know riding to school was just one of your little pretends."

"So that's all right then," said Natty.

"And Mum says she's astonished you didn't notice the chocolate cake she's made for tea, and are you coming to help eat it?"

"Yes," said Natty, looking wistfully at Ned – a pony picture once more. Jamie looked at him too.

"You're forever talking to that pony poster. That's probably why you make up such dizzy stories."

"Maybe I do and maybe I don't," said Natty with a secret smile, and giving Ned a cheery wave she set off downstairs for tea.

The End

To find out more about
Elizabeth Lindsay and her books,
visit her web site at:
www.elizabethlindsay.co.uk